·I Know You, Al·

OTHER YEARLING BOOKS YOU WILL ENJOY:

YEARLING BOOKS are designed especially to entertain
and enlighten young people. Charles F. Reasoner, Profes-
sor Emeritus of Children's Literature and Reading, New
York University, is consultant to this series.

For a complete listing of all Yearling titles, write to
Dell Publishing Co., Inc., Promotion Department,
P.O. Box 3000, Pine Brook, N.J. 07058.

·I Know You, Al·

CONSTANCE C. GREENE

Illustrated by Byron Barton

A YEARLING BOOK

Published by
Dell Publishing Co., Inc.
1 Dag Hammarskjold Plaza
New York, New York 10017

Yearling ® TM 913705, Dell Publishing Co., Inc.

ISBN: 0-440-44123-4

This edition published
by arrangement with The Viking Press, Inc.
Printed in the United States of America
Fifth Dell printing—March 1984

CW

For Cecile—
who sang the song first

· 1 ·

"WHY DO THEY CALL IT A PERIOD, IS WHAT I want to know," Al said. "Why don't they call it an exclamation point or a question mark or even a semicolon?"

Al and I were discussing getting our period. She knew perfectly well why they called it a period.

"It's for menstrual period, dummy." I am a fall guy for Al, which is maybe one reason we're such good friends. She says things like that and I rise to the bait like a first-class fish every time. Everyone we know, almost, has got her period. It's sort of like passing your driving test; when you do, people know you're grown up.

I got mine last month. Up until then, Al and I were the only two girls in our class who didn't have our period. Everybody keeps check on everybody else. I never thought it was such a big deal myself. But most of the girls I know keep their sanitary belts and pads in a package in their desks as if they might have to take a trip around the world all of a sudden and don't want to be caught short.

I never had any cramps or anything and my mother had prepared me by telling me about the ovum and the menses and the whole deal.

That left Al. And she was a whole year older than me, which made it worse. She said she didn't mind not getting her period.

"Maybe I'll never get it," she said. "After all, I'm a nonconformist. Maybe I'm such an outstanding nonconformist I'll never get my period at all. I've read that it's possible never to get it at all." The top half of her disappeared inside her locker. She thrashed around, looking for something.

"Then you can't have babies," I said. I know that your period and babies are definitely connected, but I find the facts rather hard to swallow. The facts of life, that is. I also know exactly what happens between a man and a woman to produce a baby. I know that my mother and father must have done it because here I am, not to mention my brother Teddy, fat, dumb and happy, with his mouth hanging open, as usual.

Al took me to a store once where they sell books

with pictures of men and women in ridiculous positions with no clothes on. It was enough to make you burst out laughing if you weren't sort of horrified by the whole thing. Al had been to this store before and there were a couple of pictures she especially wanted to show me. She even had the page numbers and the titles of the books written on a piece of paper. But the guy who ran the store came up to her and said, "Listen, kid, if you keep coming in here, I'm going to have to report you to the juvenile authorities. Now scram." So we had to leave without seeing the pictures.

Al shrugged her shoulders. "It's not so much, not being able to have a baby. Anyway, I don't think I'm cut out to be a mother. But of course," she said, picking at her cuticle, "there's always artificial insemination."

Once again, she had me. "What's that?"

"You never heard of artificial insemination?" Al raised her eyebrows so far they disappeared into her bangs. I don't think Al and bangs were meant for each other. She had cut them herself last week and I didn't have the heart to tell her. If she asked me, I'd say what I thought but she didn't ask.

"When a lady can't have a baby they take the sperm of an unidentified male donor and inject it into her and, presto, she's pregnant."

"You made that up," I said.

"Could I make up a story like that?" she asked me. One thing about Al, she has a very vivid imagination but she usually tells the truth.

"The only trouble," Al went on, "is that the kid might turn out to be ugly, on account of its father, the unidentified donor, was ugly or maybe a murderer or a criminal or something like that. I think you take an awful chance. Still, it's a possibility. You've got to admit that."

"Maybe the unidentified donor turns out to be handsome with a cleft in his chin," I said. "What then?"

Al looked puzzled. "What's a cleft in his chin?"

I raised my eyebrows, higher even than she could raise hers. "You don't know what a cleft in the chin is?" I asked, incredulous. "It's a sort of cavity, like a giant-sized dimple, smack in the middle of the chin. My grandfather has one. It's really nice."

"Listen." Al tugged her sweater down. "Next time your grandfather comes to visit you, let me know." She picked up her books from the windowsill.

"Have a weird day," she said and went down the hall.

It was the first time since I'd known her that Al asked the question and I had the answer ready. It was a nice feeling, for a change.

· 2 ·

AFTER SCHOOL WE WENT TO AL'S APARTMENT to do our homework, where we can have peace and quiet. Her mother works in a department store downtown. There is usually a glass jar full of carrot sticks and cucumber slices and green peppers for us to eat. Al's mother is in Better Dresses and is bugs on the subject of not eating fattening things for snacks, so she provides all these raw vegetables, which are supposed to be chock-full of vitamins and no calories.

"Have a carrot stick," Al said, tossing me one. I caught it and put it in my mouth.

"Every time I eat a carrot stick, I think of Mr. Richards," Al said. "I miss him."

Mr. Richards was the assistant superintendent of our building. He and I and Al were friends. He started giving us carrot sticks instead of bread and butter and sugar when Al went on a diet. He tried to teach us how to polish the kitchen floor the way he did. He tied rags on his feet and skated around until the floor shone, but neither one of us ever managed the trick. Mr. Richards died three months ago. Things haven't been the same since.

We were quiet for a few minutes. The sound of water dripping from the kitchen faucet was loud in the room.

"Look at what my father sent me from New Orleans," Al said. She opened a box and showed me the big, flat pieces of candy full of nuts.

"What are they?" I asked.

"Pralines. They're absolutely delicious," Al said.

"How do you know? I thought you weren't supposed to eat sweets," I said.

"The day they came, my mother said I could have one. And you know something?" Al put the box back in the cupboard. "I'm sorry I did. Before I tasted it, I didn't know how good they were. Now I know and it's a heck of a lot harder not to eat one."

"How come your father doesn't know you don't eat candy?" I said.

"How would he know? He hasn't seen me in years. I think I was eight the last time I saw him. He wouldn't recognize me if he fell over me. Except for that picture I sent him, and I've lost some weight since then." Al's father and mother are divorced. Her father sends her checks in the mail even when it isn't her birthday. He sends her postcards from all over but, so far, he hasn't come to see her. He keeps threatening but he doesn't show up. It used to bother Al a lot but now I think she's used to the idea.

The telephone rang. Al picked it up and said, "Yeah? Oh, hi, Mom. We're getting a snack. We polished off all the pralines and now we're into the mashed potatoes." She winked at me. I could hear her mother's voice, sounding high and anxious. "No, that's all right. Have a good time. I'll be fine."

Al hung up. "That was my mother. She's going out for dinner. She wanted to know if I was all right. She's got this thing about not wanting me to be alone too much. She's got a new boyfriend, in Sportswear, at the same store where she works. She's been out with him three times in the last week."

"Do you like him?"

Al shrugged. "He's O.K. At least he doesn't ask me to call him Uncle. And he doesn't give me presents to get on my good side. I'll give him that much. He probably hates me."

"Why does he hate you?"

"How would you like it if you went to take a lady out to dinner and this great big kid is sitting there giving you piercing looks. I feel as if our roles are reversed."

"What do you mean?" I said.

"It's like I'm the mother and she's the kid. I almost said, 'Don't keep her out too late, and be sure not to drive too fast.'" Al looked at herself in the mirror. "Why am I so hideous?"

"Remember what Mr. Richards said," I reminded her. "He said you were going to turn out to be a stunner someday."

"That's right, he did." Al looked pleased. "Maybe if I ran around thinking beautiful thoughts, it might help. My first beautiful thought for the day would be how nice it would be if Martha Moseley fell down and broke her leg."

We got a good laugh out of that. Martha Moseley is a girl in our class who thinks she's the world's greatest cheerleader. Martha Moseley was also the first girl in our class to get her period. You might know.

We had a few more carrot sticks and did a couple of math problems.

"I've got to go," I said. "My mother and father are going out to celebrate their anniversary and I have to brat-sit for Teddy."

"How long have your mother and father been married?"

"Fourteen years. On account of they'd been married a year and a half before I came along to brighten their life."

"Some brightener," Al said.

"You can come and help me brat-sit if you want,"
I said. "Probably it'd be all right if you came to eat
with Teddy and me."

"Not with the price of food these days," Al said.
"Besides, I've got my tuna fish and my wheat germ.
But maybe I'll come over later on."

"See you," I said.

"Fourteen years is an awful long time to be married," Al said. She looked impressed.

·3·

"MOM, YOU LOOK PRETTY GOOD," I SAID. "YOU look like you've been married four, maybe five years at the most. No one would ever guess."

"How about me?" my father said. He straightened his tie in front of the mirror. "Would they take me for a carefree bachelor?"

"More like the father of about eight kids," I said. I like my father. He is the least vain man I know.

My mother wore her taffeta dress, the one that sounds like wind rustling through tall grass. She had on her gold earrings and matching bracelet.

"Where can I possibly take you to show off all that youth and beauty?" my father said. "Why don't we just stay home? I think the ultimate anniversary celebration is to stay home with one's nearest and dearest."

My mother held out his coat. "I've got the hamburgers all set to go and there's creamed spinach and rice, if you want to cook them. The directions are on the package. The number of the restaurant is by the telephone, just in case." She kissed me. "Be kind to Teddy," she said.

"How about Teddy being kind to me?" I said. The doorbell rang. "That's Al. She's coming over to do homework."

"Happy anniversary," Al said, handing my mother a box done up in paper covered with green-and-red Santa Clauses. "It was all I had," she explained.

Mom undid the wrapping.

It was the box of candy that Al's father had sent her from New Orleans.

My mother kissed Al on the cheek. "Thank you," she said. "I love pralines."

"They're for you," Al said firmly. "I don't want any of the kids to eat your present. I want you to make sure you eat them all, both of you."

Teddy snuffled in the background. He had his hand out, ready to rip one off but Al gave him such a piercing look he scratched his nose instead, pretending that was what he planned to do all along.

"Your mother looks super," Al said when they'd gone.

"My father looks super too."

"Your father is a prince."

I didn't argue with her. I cooked the hamburgers and toasted rolls, so I wouldn't have to cook rice. They got a little scorched. I scraped off the scorched part but still Teddy gagged and carried on.

"Grow up," I told him.

"I heard a song today," Teddy announced. "A dirty song."

"Better run out to the hall and check to see if they're gone," Al said.

"My bonnie lies over the ocean," Teddy sang, "My bonnie lies over the sea, My father lay over my mother, and that is how I came to be."

Al and I looked at each other. I went on eating my hamburger, and Al got herself a glass of water.

"How'd you like that?" Teddy said. "You want me to sing it again?"

Neither of us answered him. We went on eating and drinking. "I think I'll wear my blue sweater tomorrow," Al said, pushing back her bangs. "It makes me feel so sexy."

Teddy repeated the song, from start to finish. He didn't miss a beat. "You get it?" he asked us when he'd finished.

"You think he's ready for the other thing?" Al asked me.

"What other thing?"

"You know. What we were talking about in school today. The a-r-t-i-f-i-c-i-a-l i-n-s-e-m-i-n-a-t-i-o-n."

Al is a much better speller than I am.

Teddy's head swiveled on his neck like he was watching a tennis match.

"Spell it again," he said, "slower."

"Heck, no, I don't think he's ready for that," I said. "I'm not ready—how could he be?"

"Sorry, Ted," Al said. "You'll have to wait a couple of years. Tough luck. Keep on trying."

Teddy was practically in tears. "A kid told me it was a very dirty song," he wailed. "Don't you think it is?"

"It'll do until something better comes along," Al said.

Teddy looked crestfallen. I felt so sorry for him I didn't even make him finish his creamed spinach. It went into the dog's dish, along with the scorched roll. Teddy is a very picky eater, as I may have mentioned before.

"Why don't you go drown your sorrows in the bathtub, kid?" I said to him. "You can take your ark and all the animals in with you, and I'll even let you have a little of Mom's bath salts."

Teddy cheered up a bit at that. My mother has the pink bath salts that smell like geraniums, which Teddy is a pushover for. "The only trouble is," he said the last time I let him use them, "it hurts when I sit on it. It sticks me in my rear end."

I clued him in about letting the hot water melt the

stuff, then it wouldn't stick him, and that made things O.K. When you're only nine, getting joy out of life is very easy. It's only as you grow up that it becomes more difficult.

We listened at the door as Teddy filled the tub. He sang "My bonnie lies over the ocean" at the top of his voice.

"That was mean," Al said. "Here he thought he was such a hotshot bringing home a dirty song, and we didn't even react."

"I'll get him to sing it next time my mother has a tea party," I said. "That ought to get a reaction of some sort."

After a while Al said she had to go. "You didn't say anything about my bangs," she added.

"I didn't notice," I said.

"As a liar, you finish last," she said. She put her hand on her forehead, pushing the bangs down so far they covered her eyebrows.

"Who beat down that brow?" she said, looking at herself in the mirror. Then she crossed her eyes at me, picked up her books, and opened the door.

"Have a weird day, what's left of it," she said.

"I'll try," I said. "See you tomorrow."

· 4 ·

NEXT MORNING WHEN WE MET IN THE LOBBY I could see that Al didn't have on her blue sweater after all. Instead, she had on a brown vest that she wears only when she's feeling mean. That brown vest is a danger signal.

I decided not to ask what was wrong. She'd tell me when she was good and ready.

"It was bizarre," Al said when we got to the corner.

"What was?" I asked, trying to spell "bizarre" in my head.

"You know I told you my mother was going out with a man from Sportswear?" Al said. We waited for the light to change. People passing us on the street had the gray, fuzzy look they usually had in the morning. I don't know whether they actually were gray and fuzzy or whether it was the sleep still in my eyes. Probably both.

"Yeah," I said, waiting. "You said she'd been out with him twice already this week."

"Three times," Al said sternly. "Well, I fell asleep and when I woke up, the light was still on in the living room and I felt as if I'd been asleep for hours—you know the way you do—so I got up to see if she was home."

The sign changed to WALK and Al and I crossed the street. I could hardly wait to get to the other side.

"She was kissing him and he was kissing her back. And I mean he was kissing her!" Al looked at me out of the corner of her eye. "They didn't even hear me come in. So I backed out as fast as I could and went back to bed. I hardly slept at all after that." Al hugged her books against her chest as if she were trying to keep warm.

"And let me tell you, it was the kind of kissing that can only lead to one thing."

I thought of Teddy singing his song and of the pictures I'd seen of the sex act. Or what leads up to the sex act. I wanted to ask if Al's mother and her new boyfriend had their clothes on or off, but I figured that would be going too far. We are best friends but there are some things even best friends don't discuss.

"What could it lead to?" I finally asked.

"I don't *believe* you," Al said. She stopped smack in the middle of the sidewalk and stared at me. "*Marriage*, that's what it could lead to. I wouldn't be at all surprised if she got married." We started walking again.

"That might not be too bad," I said. Al's mother getting married had been the furthest thing from my mind. "Then you'd have a father."

I put my foot in it then, I knew. Al sort of raised her shoulders and I could almost see the ice forming on her ears. "I already have a perfectly good father," she said. "Why should I want another one?"

"He wouldn't be your father, he'd be your half father, or your stepfather," I said, trying to repair the damage. "They say stepfathers are really nice, sometimes nicer than real fathers."

Al didn't answer me. When we got to the gym door, Martha Moseley was standing there with her two cronies, Linda Benton and Sally Sykes. Linda Benton and Sally Sykes are as close to being nothing as any two girls I've ever known. I don't think they go to the bathroom without asking Martha if it's O.K. with her. I don't know why somebody like Martha has the power over people she seems to have. Last year two other girls practically laid down their coats when they came to a puddle so Martha wouldn't get her feet wet. Martha Moseley is probably the biggest phony God ever put on this earth.

Martha looked over her shoulder at us.

"I've got a note from my mother," she said, like she was the lead in the school play and wanted to be sure her voice carried to the last row. "To excuse me from playing basketball. I've got my period again."

Linda and Sally looked at each other and then at us as if they were thinking of calling an ambulance.

"Poor M," Linda said. They called her M when they were being super super slobs. "When she gets her period she's absolutely knocked out."

"Hey, wow," Al said in a loud voice. "Too bad she doesn't get it more often. Then she'd be unconscious all the time instead of just some of the time."

Al and I marched past them into the hall. It was lucky Martha didn't have a loaded weapon on her or she would've unloaded it in our direction. Linda and Sally both dropped their mouths open so they resembled Teddy, which is a terrible thing to say about anyone.

"I'll say this," Al said when we got to our lockers and started unloading our stuff, "I started out the day feeling lousy. But now I feel pretty good."

There was a peculiar smell in my locker. I think I must've shoved either my dirty gym socks or part of a sandwich in the back and forgotten about it.

"What's that terrible smell?" Al asked.

"Maybe I'll check on it this afternoon. It's almost time now for the bell."

Al looked down at her brown vest. "I should've worn my blue sweater."

"Wear it tomorrow," I said.

"Suppose he asks me for her hand," Al said.

"What?"

"Her hand. Suppose he asks me for my mother's hand in marriage. Seeing as I'm her daughter, maybe he'll ask me for my permission to marry my mother." Al slammed her locker door. "I saw a movie on TV last week where the father of the girl asks the suitor what his prospects are—how much money he makes and how much he expects to make. Can he provide for his daughter, stuff like that."

"Isn't that kind of old-fashioned?" I said.

"Maybe." Al looked doubtful. "Why don't you check with your mother and father, find out if he asked for your mother's hand. I mean, I'm the only person this guy could ask, when you come right down to it."

"It sounds kind of nervy to me," I said. "A kid your age asking a grown man how much money he makes. I don't think he'd like that at all. It's really none of your business."

Al stuck out her lower lip and blew up at her bangs to get them out of her eyes.

"I'll tell you one thing," she said as the bell rang, "they better not ask me to go on their honeymoon with them."

"Why would they do that?" I asked her.

Al picked up her books. "They might feel sorry for me," she said. "They might feel sorry for me because I was going to be alone. It won't bother me to stay alone. I'm used to it."

"Sure," I said, opening the door to our homeroom. "Anyway, you always have me."

· 5 ·

"LISTEN, MOM," I SAID THAT NIGHT WHEN I was peeling potatoes, "did Dad ask Grandfather for your hand when you decided to get married? Did he want to know how much money Dad made?"

My mother was on her hands and knees with her head stuck under the sink looking for some soap. "Your father was making seventy-five dollars a week and I was making ninety," she said. "It was sort of embarrassing. I told him he could lie and say he was making ninety, too, but he wouldn't do it. Why do you ask?"

"I just wanted to know," I said, gouging at a black spot with the point of the potato peeler. "It's an old-fashioned custom, right?" I said. "Nobody does it anymore."

"From what I understand," my mother said, sitting back on her heels, "there is nothing that nobody *doesn't* do. Young people only get married nowadays after they've been living together to try it for size. I think it's sad, never mind the morality of it. Morality is an outmoded word, I'm afraid."

"Al's mother isn't young," I said. "Does living together and sleeping together mean the same thing?"

"One usually leads to the other," she answered. "What's on your mind?"

"Well, Al's mother has this new boyfriend, and Al thinks maybe they're going to get married." I left out the part about them kissing because maybe Al wouldn't want me to tell that. "And Al thinks he might ask her for her mother's hand in marriage and she might have to ask him what his prospects are, how much money he makes, and I told her I thought that would be sort of fresh."

My mother whistled softly.

"Right on," she said. She gets hold of expressions like that from reading the papers and watching TV, and when she gets attached to a certain expression she won't let go.

"And Al thinks they're going to ask her to go on their honeymoon with them because they'll feel sorry about leaving her alone. Can we ask her to stay with us?"

"Why don't you wait and see what happens?" my

mother said. "Maybe they're only platonic friends, Al's mother and this man."

"That's all you know," I said. Sometimes you have to protect your parents from the hard facts.

The bell rang and it was Al standing in the hall.

"Did you ask yet?" she whispered.

"Yeah," I said. "She said my father was making seventy-five bucks a week and she was making ninety, so it was sort of embarrassing, but he wouldn't lie about how much he was making. She said follow the wait-and-see policy."

"He's there now," Al said darkly. "They're having a cocktail. He gave me the business about what grade was I in, what was my favorite subject, etcetera. I was watching a special about Bermuda on the telly and he asked me if I'd ever been there. I said no and he said he had and it was beautiful. Then you know what he said?" Al peered out from behind her bangs at me. They seemed to have grown since that afternoon.

"No. What?" I am basically a straight-man type.

She looked over her shoulder to make sure no one was around. "He said too bad, I'd have to go there someday."

I thought that one over.

"So?" I said. "So what?"

She poked me in the chest.

"Bermuda. What's Bermuda famous for? You don't know?" She didn't even give me a chance to answer.

"Honeymoons, wimp. That's what Bermuda's famous for. Honeymoons."

"Listen, if he didn't offer you a free airplane ticket on the spot, forget it." I was trying to make her feel better but things did not look good.

"It's O.K. for you to say," she said. "I've been thinking. I might join the Army. I just finished watching a TV commercial about all the advantages the Army has to offer women."

"There's only one thing wrong with that," I said.

"What?" she said.

For the second time I had the answer to Al's question.

"You ain't no woman, baby," I said.

We got a good laugh out of that and Al zapped down the hall to her apartment to keep an eye on things.

· 6 ·

WHEN I RANG HER BELL SATURDAY MORNING
Al came to the door still in her pajamas. She had an
old towel wrapped around her head, pulled straight
across her forehead and tucked behind her ears. She
looked sort of like an Egyptian pharaoh with glasses.

"I've got to do a load of wash," I said. "Come with
me?"

"I can't," she said, breathing heavily, "I'm doing
needlepoint."

"I didn't know you knew how to do needlepoint."

"I don't. My mother brought this eyeglass case
home for me to start on, which is driving me up the
walls. But I'm going to finish it if it kills me."

"Five'll get you ten it will," I said. I don't understand odds but I like the way they sound. Al doesn't
understand them either, which is good.

She waved her hands around. "I'm doing it as a lesson in self-discipline," she said. "It's good for you to do things you hate doing."

"It is?" I had started to knit a sweater when I was about ten. It made me so nervous I felt like jumping out the window. My mother finished it for me. One sleeve was longer than the other, and when I tried to pull the thing over my head, I almost choked to death. My mother put it in a hot-water wash and it came out looking just about right for a six-month-old baby. We were both relieved.

"Then after I do my needlepoint, I have to clean up my room," Al said. "My mother wants me to go down to the store and meet her and you-know-who. He's taking us to lunch."

"Has he got a name?" I asked her.

Al wrinkled her nose. "His name is Mr. Lynch. Mr. Henry Lynch. He's pretty old, about forty-five or so. He wears after-shave lotion. Very powerful after-shave lotion. And he wears a gold ring on his pinkie. Does that tell you anything?" Al stared at me.

"As long as he doesn't wear an earring in one ear, so what's to worry?" I said. We know this boy who wears an earring in one ear. He's a real wimp but he thinks he's a hot dog. A wimp who thinks he's a hot dog is one of the most pathetic people going.

"Why have you got that on your head?" I asked, pointing to the towel.

"When I started the needlepoint my bangs kept getting in my eyes, so I put this on to keep 'em out," Al said.

"Any news? About last night, I mean. Anything new on Bermuda?" I asked.

I should've known. Al likes to tell things in her own good time. Lucky for me the phone rang just then, because she started to get that expression on her face that made me think I made Bermuda up.

"Go answer it," I said. "It's probably somebody calling to tell you you're a missing heir."

Meanwhile I looked at the fashion magazines Al's mother gets, due to her job working in Better Dresses. They are far out. The girls look as if they have stilts for legs.

Al's voice sounded high and not like her at all. I heard her say, "I guess that'll be all right. Do you want me to come down there? . . . O.K. I'll have to clue my mother in. See you."

She came to the door of the living room. She looked white and funny.

"Who was that?" I asked. Maybe somebody really *had* told her she'd inherited some money.

"It was my father," Al said, in a trance. She sat down on the sofa very carefully. "He's here. He's staying in a hotel. He wants me to have dinner with him, Tonight." We looked at each other.

When Al and I first became friends, she used to

think every airplane flying overhead might be bringing her father to see her. But she was older now and hadn't mentioned him in quite a while.

"No kidding!" I said. "That's great. Terrific."

Al started thumping her fist on the table so hard the ashtrays bounced.

"Who does he think he is?" she shouted. "Who does he think he is that he can forget about me for almost six years and then all of a sudden decide to give me a big treat and take me out for dinner? I don't think I'll go. When he shows up, I'll have my mother tell him I have a fungus or the mange or something."

"What will your mother say when she hears he's coming?" I asked.

"She thinks people who get divorced should be civilized about it," Al said as if she was reciting a lesson. "She says divorce is a fact of life. But you know something?"

I shook my head.

She looked at the wall over the sofa and she wasn't paying any attention to me. "If I ever got a divorce from my husband after we have a kid and all that junk, and I had loved him, I wouldn't be civilized about it. Boy, if he walked out on me and my kid, I'd be sore. Good and sore."

She started to stomp around the room, stiff-legged, the way she does when she's burned up about something.

"I don't think I'll go out to dinner with him," she said.

"I know you, Al," I told her. I tried to get her to smile. "You'll go—anything for a free meal. Now get back to your needlepoint and blow your brains out. See if I care."

I'm happy to say that got her laughing. She came out in the hall in her pajamas and her Egyptian pharaoh's headdress. While we were waiting for the elevator, she did a little belly dance. We both want to take lessons in belly dancing but so far haven't asked our mothers.

When the elevator stopped at our floor, a man and lady got out. They looked at Al in a very disapproving way. She scuttled back inside.

"Stay loose," I told her.

"Have a weird day," she said.

Then I went down to do the wash.

·7·

I WAS GOING TO TAKE THE CROSSTOWN BUS TO
see my friend Polly Peterson, but it started to rain
cats and dogs and my mother said I'd better call
Polly and tell her I'd come some other time. Polly
moved away about the same time Al moved into our
building. Polly and I were good friends but not as
good friends as Al and I are. Polly is my second best
friend. We both cried when she had to move and
vowed we'd be best friends forever. But that lasted
about two weeks and now she has a best friend named
Thelma.

Polly is very skinny and scrawny and she got her
period when she was ten. Her mother is the kind
who believes in giving kids the facts of life practically
before they're able to walk, so Polly was the one who

told me how babies were born. I told her she was a liar and started to hit her, and she told me I was a baby. We didn't speak to each other for a day and a half. Anyway, Polly knew everything there was to know. So when she got her period and it was over, she said to her mother, "Boy, I'm glad that's over," and her mother had to explain that it was just the beginning. Polly had thought, so you get your period, you have it once, and that was that. Polly is a riot.

There's nothing worse than a rainy Saturday, especially when you live in an apartment and your best friend is having lunch in a restaurant with her mother and her mother's boyfriend. Not to mention she's also going out to dinner with her long-lost father. Teddy was down in 12-C visiting a wimpy little friend of his and my mother and father were at a building committee meeting. There've been a lot of complaints lately about litter outside the building, and people are up in arms. One old lady stepped in a dog turd and almost got a concussion when she skidded on it, so they're having a meeting to decide what to do. My father said, "Dogs will be dogs," but my mother made him go anyway.

I went through my mother's bureau drawers to see if there were any additions or anything I'd missed the last time. There weren't. Then I went through her jewelry box and put on a pair of dangly earrings and a touch of blue eyeshadow.

I half closed my eyes and made a sexy face.

"I vant to be alone," I said. Nobody argued with me.

The rain was coming down so hard I couldn't even see across the courtyard. I decided to dust the bookshelf Mr. Richards had helped me make. I keep it in my bedroom. I polished it really well and I even took out all the books first. Then I sat down on my bed, closed my eyes and sent a couple of very strong thought waves up to Mr. Richards. I told him Al and I thought about him a lot. I also told him the new super was a slob and lazy to boot. I wonder if Mr. Richards is whipping around heaven, rags tied to his sneakers, showing St. Peter how to shine the linoleum.

"Glide, glide!" I can hear him shouting. Even if he was talking to St. Peter, he'd still yell. Mr. Richards is not the kind of person who would be impressed by who someone was.

After I got over my first really sad feeling about Mr. Richards' dying, I thought about how nice it was to have known him, about all the good times he and Al and I had. He taught us how to make soup and cream sauce and crepes suzette, and I never have a Coke without hearing him say, "How about a shooter of Coke?" Mr. Richards had been a bartender before he was assistant super. He was what my grandmother would call "a rare soul," and I'm glad I knew him even for a little while. Al feels the same way.

I looked at the clock for about the fourteenth time.

It was only one thirty. I turned on the television and got semi-engrossed in an old Tarzan movie. My mother and father came in from the meeting with my father muttering about how he'd never go to another one. My mother told him sternly he had to have some sense of responsibility. Sometimes she talks to him just the way she talks to Teddy and me.

"We're going over to the Babcocks' tonight," my mother said. "Maybe you'd like to have Al over."

"I would but she can't come. She's having dinner with her father," I said.

My mother raised her eyebrows. "Her father? How exciting! She must be thrilled. When did he show up?"

"He called this morning," I told her. "Mostly, Al's sore. She says who does he think he is to show up after all these years and expect her to be all suited up ready to go out for a hamburger."

"Something's gone bad in the refrigerator," my father said, helping himself to a beer. He was always giving my mother a hard time about stuff that got shoved to the back and started to smell.

She ignored him.

"Yes," she said, "I can see that might be her reaction. Still, I remember how she longed for him to come and see her when she first moved in. Her feelings about him are ambivalent."

"What's that mean?" I asked.

"Well, she wants to see him but, on the other hand, she's resentful toward him. For leaving her and her mother. She feels both positive and negative about him."

"I'm pretty ambivalent about you too," my father said. "Most of the time I think you're smashing. It's only when I get a whiff of some of the goodies in the refrigerator that I'm not so sure."

"Hadn't you better shave if we're going to the Babcocks'?" my mother said in a frosty tone.

"All the Babcocks talk about is people we don't know," my father complained.

My mother gave him what Al would call "a piercer." My father would just as soon stay home on Saturday night and watch the Mary Tyler Moore show, but my mother says she can stay home and watch TV any night.

"But not Mary," he says every time. He knows he'll wind up going to the Babcocks' but he's a man who believes in trying.

"Does Teddy have to stay here?" I said.

"No," she said, very slowly and clearly, "the Babcocks would be mad about having a nine-year-old boy around all evening."

"Maybe Teddy knows some of the people the Babcocks talk about all the time that I don't know," my father said hopefully. "Why don't we send him over instead of us?"

· 8 ·

THE SECOND MY MOTHER AND FATHER WENT
to the Babcocks', Teddy started in. First, he had to
call his friend Hubie about some spelling words.
Then he wanted a piece of lemon meringue pie he
knew perfectly well was for Sunday dinner. When
I put the kibosh on everything, he started whining
about a composition he had to write for English about
what he'd do to clean up the city.

"Put all the dogs in a giant kennel," I said, "and
only let them out every six months or so. Stop all
cars at the city limits and make people take the bus
or subway from there on. How's that for starters?"

"How about if I invent a gigantic vacuum cleaner
that sucks up all the garbage and fumes and everything?" Teddy said. "Then give every person a horse
to ride to work."

Sometimes Teddy surprises me. He really does.

"Why don't you sit down and write that instead of making noise?" I told him. "Those are two good ideas."

One kind word and that kid takes off like a 707. That's the trouble with him. If you keep a foot firmly in the middle of his back and snarl at him regularly, he stays in line. But tell him something nice, he's atrocious. He started mincing around the room, pretending he was trying out for the Miss Junior High of America contest. He twirled an imaginary baton, tossing it up in the air and down between his legs. Baton twirling is very big in those contests. Actually, Teddy would be quite amusing if he were somebody else's little brother. It's when you have to live in the same house with him, day to day, that he gets you down.

"There's Al!" he shouted when the bell rang. I told him Al said she'd stop in so I could see how she looked for her dinner date. Teddy likes Al because she gives him the time of day. Being an only child herself, she has more patience with him than I do.

"Ta-dah," Al said when I opened the door.

"Say it like you meant it," I told her. Usually she throws her arms wide, as if she were announcing a big event. Tonight she just sort of said it like "So what?"

"You look nice," I told her. Her cheeks were pink and her eyes were sparkling and she'd probably have to go to the bathroom about a thousand times, she was so nervous.

"I look like a frankfurter stuffed into a bun that's too small for it," she said. "A sale purchase of my mother's. What do you think?"

She had on a suit, I guess you'd call it, or a two-piece dress. It had a pleated skirt and a middy top. I couldn't decide whether it was too old or too young for Al.

"It makes your rear end stick out," Teddy said. I could've smacked him. I did. Not hard. He only yelped a little. Teddy has a thing about rear ends sticking out. At his age.

"That's what I thought," Al said dismally. She sat down. "I can only stay a minute. He's coming at six. I heard my mother tell Ole Henry not to come for her until seven. I brought my needlepoint. I figure I'm on the verge of a nervous breakdown anyway. What's one more push toward the abyss?"

"Hey, can I try?" Teddy asked.

"Nah, Ted," she said, "you don't want to do needlepoint."

"Sure I do," Teddy insisted. Anything you tell him he doesn't want to do, he automatically wants to do ten times more than before you told him he didn't want to.

"It's very hard," Al said. "But I will say when it's finished it's worth the effort."

She moved over on the couch and Teddy sat down

beside her. "This is the way it goes," Al said, handing him the eyeglass case and the needle. "You just stick it in this hole, pull it through, then stick it in from behind and pull it through again."

Teddy turned out to be a natural at needlepoint.

"How'm I doing?" he'd holler every time he completed a stitch and Al would check his work.

"For a boy, you're not bad," she said. Teddy beamed.

"I like it," he kept saying. "I really like doing needlepoint."

"How was lunch?" I asked Al.

She shrugged. "O.K. Ole Henry said I could have whatever I wanted so I had an avocado stuffed with shrimp and a hot fudge sundae. He's not so bad."

Al and I watched television while Teddy relaxed over Al's needlepoint. She kept going to the door and peering into the hall. "I thought I heard the elevator," she said.

"You did the kid a big favor," I said. "He was all clutched up before you got here about writing a composition for English. Now he's as soft as a grape."

"I wish I was Teddy's age again," Al said wistfully. "Life was pretty simple back in those days." She got up and started to walk around the edges of the living-room rug.

"You know something?" she said, putting one foot directly in front of the other, going round and round, not looking at me. "I'm getting awful tired of wait-ing."

"Waiting?" I said. I thought she meant for her father.

"Yes." Al sounded angry. "I'm tired of waiting to be good looking. I'm tired of waiting to be popular. I'm tired of waiting to get my period."

Al was almost crying. Most of the time she doesn't get emotional.

Teddy stopped doing Al's needlepoint.

"What's she mean, her period?" he asked me.

"It's O.K., Ted," I said. "Why don't you go into the kitchen and whip up one of your famous sodas? There's coffee ice cream in the freezer."

Teddy wanted to know what was up but all you have to do to divert that kid is say "ice cream" and he wouldn't hang around to find out where Captain Kidd's treasure is buried. He made a big racket in the kitchen, opening and shutting doors. There'd be a mess when he was through.

I sat beside Al on the couch. "Relax," I said. "You'll probably have a neat time tonight and find lots of things to talk about to him."

"It's not just seeing my father," Al said. "It's every-thing. My mother, Ole Henry, the works. The world is too much with me," she said. I guess I looked dumb. "That's a line from a poem I like. It says what I feel."

She put out her hand and almost touched my arm.

"What would you think about going to live in a commune?" she asked me suddenly.

"Well," I said, "I guess it'd be all right. I don't know. I never thought about it much. One thing, you'd have a ready-made family. Everybody takes care of the babies together and they share the work and everything."

"Yeah," Al said. Her mouth turned down. "I guess I better split."

"It's only twenty to," I said, looking at the clock.

"I better go. I want to be home when he gets there. You know." Al stuffed her needlepoint in her pocket. We went to the door.

"The one thing about a commune is you eat all that organic food and stuff. And no meat. They're practically all vegetarians. I don't think I'd like that." She looked out at me from behind her bangs. I didn't know what to say.

Al put her head down as if she was trying to tuck it between her shoulders. I was glad she didn't have any farther to go than down the hall. I waited until she went into her apartment before I closed the door. She didn't say "Have a weird day" or anything.

I watched at the door for a long time, trying to catch a glimpse of her father but I must've missed him.

·9·

I WANTED TO CALL AL FIRST THING SUNDAY morning to find out how things had gone but my mother wouldn't let me.

"Let well enough alone," she said. Whatever *that* means. "I'm sure Al will be in touch when she's ready."

The sun was shining. I could actually see a sliver of fantastically blue sky between buildings when I looked out the window. It was a good day to be alive. I hope Al thought so too. Polly called and asked me for lunch. I felt as if I were deserting Al. She might want to have a heart-to-heart. On the other hand, Sunday was togetherness day at her house. It was the only day her mother had completely free. She liked Al to stick around so they could do things. Sometimes Al thought it was a drag. Not always. Probably from now on Ole Henry would be part of the togetherness, thus throwing Al into a real pit of depression.

When I got to Polly's, the kitchen was a shambles because she was fixing lunch. Polly wanted to go to the Cordon Bleu, which is a really fancy cooking school. She snorted when people said all the really great chefs of the world were men. Polly planned on being a really great chef.

"Long time no see," Polly said, chopping onions and garlic and shallots like a mad woman and throwing them in a pan. She started chopping all that stuff before she knew how to boil an egg. As a matter of fact, she still couldn't boil an egg. That easy cooking didn't interest her. The place smelled strong but good. She had on a huge billowing apron. All I could see of Polly was her hands and feet. She had what my mother called "an interesting face." Which meant she wasn't pretty and probably never would be, but when she got old, like around forty, she'd be better than pretty. She had straight blond hair, green eyes, and lots of bones. Everybody has bones, I know, but Polly seemed to have more than most people. Her eyes slanted a little. She looked sort of like a skinny, aristocratic cat.

"I was hoping you might bring Al," Polly said. She and Al had hit it off right from the start. "I should've said to. I'm inventing a new kind of omelet and there's going to be plenty."

"Al's father showed up to take her out for dinner last night," I said.

"Super," Polly said. "She must be beside herself with joy."

"She is in a pit," I said. "She says who does he think he is to just come as if he'd never been away. Not only that, she hasn't got her period yet, and she's the only one in the class who hasn't. She says she's sick of waiting for things to happen. She thinks her mother might get married to Ole Henry, and he wears after-shave lotion and a ring on his pinkie."

"Bad news," Polly said, stirring.

"What's going on with you?" I said, sitting on a kitchen stool. The Petersons have all kinds of odd looking pots and pans hanging on their walls. Mr. Peterson is in the diplomatic service and has been posted in France and Egypt, among other places.

"Life is very dull," Polly said. "Evelyn came home last weekend from Boston and said she's thinking of getting married. My mother says we never should have let her go to New England in the first place."

Evelyn is Polly's sister. She has even more bones than Polly. She is twenty and studying to be a ballerina. She has been living with boys ever since she was eighteen. Polly's mother and father are very progressive, or liberal, however you want to call it.

The first time Evelyn came home and said she was living with a boy, the only one who got excited was Polly.

"Evelyn's got to put herself on a pedestal," Polly told me. She was only eleven at the time and still believed in women being put on pedestals. Polly read a lot about the early days of our country when I guess this was not unusual. Anyway, the guy Evelyn was living with had lost some teeth in an accident and he had a set of false ones, which he used to flip in and out, and that got on her nerves.

The strangest thing about me and Polly being friends is that my family is so conservative and hers is so far out. I guess that's what attracted us to each other in the first place.

"Who's she thinking of marrying?" I said, helping myself to an olive. "The one with the dentures?"

"No." Polly beat up a couple of eggs as if she was mad at them. "This one is studying to be a lawyer. His family is very proper, and my mother says she doesn't think it'll work. Basically," Polly said, wiping her hands on the front of her apron, "my mother is against marriage."

"She is?" Polly's mother is a weirdo but nice.

"She's thinking of changing her name back to what it was before she married my father, but he says too much water has gone over the dam or under the bridge. He's not sure which. He says she'd lose her credibility if she did that. My mother is just getting warmed up. No telling where she'll end." Polly slid the eggs into the pan with all the other stuff and turned the heat down low.

"My mother says she doesn't think Evelyn should get married to anyone for a long time. She also doesn't think she should keep living with different people."

"She doesn't?" I watched while she slid the eggs around in the pan gently until all of a sudden they looked just right, then flipped them out on a plate with all the onions and stuff in the middle. I tried to do this myself once but the whole thing turned into a disaster. "I thought you said your mother was against marriage," I said as we sat down and started to eat. "It's delicious," I told Polly.

"It needs salt," she said. "My mother isn't against marriage per se. She doesn't think Evelyn is ready for marriage. That's why she said we never should have let her go to New England where people get married a lot. She says New Englanders are superconservative. She thinks Evelyn should settle on one person and live with him for a few years until she is ready for a more permanent relationship. But you know Evelyn." Polly shook her head. "She'll do what she wants to do and woe to anyone who stands in her way. If she does marry this guy from Boston, I feel sort of sorry for him. You know?"

I nodded. I felt sorry for him too. "How's Thelma?" I said.

Polly put her head on one side. "Thelma's getting

kind of uppity," she said. "Her zits cleared up due to some miracle salve her dermatologist gave her, and she lost five pounds from around her waist, and guess where they went?"

"Don't tell me," I said.

"Right. Those five little old pounds traveled from Thelma's waist right up to her chest and stayed there. Boys started calling her up and everything. If I lost five pounds from around my waist, they'd go straight to my ankles like a homing pigeon."

"And if I lost five pounds from my waist, they'd go to my ears or my fingers or my knees," I said.

"If you lost five pounds from anywhere, they'd haul you off to the SPCC and arrest your mother and father for not feeding you enough," Polly said.

"You should talk," I said. We laughed for about five minutes and then decided we'd better clean up the pots and pans before Polly's mother and father got home.

"That's the worst thing about cooking, the cleaning up," I said.

"When I get to be one of the world's great chefs, I won't have to clean up," Polly said, scraping out the frying pan.

"How come?" I said.

"A great chef doesn't scrub pots and pans, any more than a queen scrubs out the bathtub," Polly said haughtily. "There are plenty of menials around to do the dirty work. Are you ready for dessert?"

Polly had made a torte, which is a very rich cake with nuts, and put it on the table.

"It didn't rise very well," I said.

"It's not supposed to rise. There's no flour in it. It's supposed to be like that—all flat."

I tasted it. "Not bad," I said. I prefer ordinary cake but I didn't want to hurt her feelings. "Polly," I said, "do you know about artificial insemination?"

"Artificial *what?*" Polly said.

"It's when a lady can't have a baby, so they get some unidentified male donor and shoot his sperm into the lady and, presto, she's pregnant," I told her.

"You're out of your tree," Polly said. "I never heard of such a thing. Why don't they just do it the old-fashioned way?"

"I told you," I said, very patient. "The lady can't have a baby the normal way so that's what they do. It's a sort of last resort, I guess."

"I should hope so," Polly said indignantly. "That's the dumbest thing I ever heard of. Who told you?"

"Al did. She read it somewhere. Al is very up on things like that. We were talking about if she never got her period and she couldn't have a baby, and she said she didn't think she was cut out to be a mother, and that's when she told me."

"I'm going to ask my mother," Polly said. I could see she was put out that her mother hadn't told her, that I knew something she didn't know.

"Maybe your mother doesn't know about it," I said. "I guess it's the latest thing."

The clock the Petersons had brought home from the Hague where Mr. Peterson was posted before Polly was born boomed out four times.

"I better get going," I said, "or my mother will be on the horn to find out if I've started."

The telephone rang.

"Tell her I just left," I said, one hand on the doorknob.

"Oh, hello, how are you?" Polly said in a juicy voice. "She just left. I hear the elevator going down now. O.K., see you soon."

She hung up. "You just left," she said. We went out in the hall and rang for the elevator.

"Next time you come over to my house and I'll fix lunch," I said. "We'll have my famous peanut-butter surprise and I'll ask Al to come too."

Polly said that'd be great. She grabbed me and kissed me on both cheeks, the way the French do.

"Have a weird day," I said, borrowing Al's line. The elevator had stopped and the doors were open. I guess my voice was pretty loud. There were a bunch of people inside. They laughed like crazy. When the doors closed I just faced the front of the car and pretended I wasn't there. When we got to the lobby, I was the first one out.

Sometimes grown-ups can be very rude.

·10·

"AL'S BEEN TRYING TO GET YOU ALL AFTER-
noon," my mother said when I got home. "I told her
you'd call the minute you got in."

The words were barely out of her mouth before
our bell rang. Al was leaning against the door when
I opened it and practically fell into the room.

"Hey, baby," I said, "come on in."

Al looked as if she were about to go up in smoke.
My mother said, "Why don't you girls go into your
room so you can talk without being interrupted?"
Sometimes my mother is extremely tactful.

I led the way down the hall. Behind me, I could
hear Al breathing. I shut the door and said, "O.K.
Tell me about it. How was your father?"

She waved her arms and started pacing. "If you

hadn't been home this time I would've hurled myself from the roof," she said. "If I had to wait one more minute to tell you, I might've burst right through my epidermis and messed up the entire apartment with my guts. You won't believe what I have to tell you." Her eyes were wild and she didn't stop moving.

"It's the most bizarre thing that ever happened. Absolutely the most bizarre event of my life."

"You got your period," I said.

Al wasn't listening. Her eyes shone at me through her bangs. In a minute she'd probably have to go to the bathroom. Whenever she gets excited, she has to go.

"Wait a sec." She went to the bathroom.

"I can't get over it," she said when she came out, picking up where she'd left off, without missing a beat.

"My mother is absolutely flabbergasted. Even Ole Henry is flabbergasted and he doesn't flabbergast easy."

"How does he know?" I asked.

"He was there when I got home last night."

"You clued Ole Henry in about getting your period?" I said. I thought that was a bit too much togetherness.

"What?" Al stared at me. She started to track. "Who said I got my period?"

"I thought that's what you were talking about," I said.

"Anyone can get a period," Al said loftily. "What happened to me is astronomical compared to that."

I didn't think she meant astronomical but I didn't want to interrupt her. As if I could've. She was wound up and nothing was going to stop her.

"Listen," I said, "sit down and tell me what happened. Take a deep breath. Pull yourself together."

Al sat down on my bed, then bounced up and started to pace again.

"What's your father like?" I said.

Al put her hands on her hips. "He is really quite a nice-looking man," she said seriously. "He is older looking than I remembered him."

"What'd your mother say when she saw him?" That's what I really wanted to know. I wish I could've been there when he came to pick up Al for their dinner date.

"She said, 'Hello, Charles, how are you?' She asked him to sit down and he said no thanks, and he helped me on with my coat."

I waited. I can be quite patient at times. I knew Al wasn't going to be hurried.

"He said, 'You're looking very well, Virginia.' "

"I didn't know your mother's name was Virginia," I said. "I thought it was Vi." Once in a while Al and I call our mothers by their first names, just for laughs.

"He called her Virginia, which she hates," Al said. "She said 'Thank you, Charles.' " Al put her head to one side, like a bird. "They sounded sort of, you know, sort of like people do in a soap opera. They didn't sound real."

"Where'd you go for dinner?"

"He told me to suggest a place because he was a stranger around here, so I took him to Belucchio's and I had a sausage pizza and he had manicotti half and half. He had a glass of wine and I had spumoni. Then he had another glass of wine and he said, 'You're probably wondering why I'm here after all this time,' and I looked him straight in the eye and said, 'Yes, Dad, I am.'"

"Good for you," I said. "That was socking it to him. That was very good."

Al smiled at me. "I was sort of proud of myself," she admitted. "It made me feel better. And then you know what I said?"

I shook my head.

"I said, 'I wish you'd come sooner.'"

"And what'd he say?"

"He said, 'I'm sorry, Al, I wish I had too.'" Al looked at her hands and then at me. "I felt sorry for him. I think it took a lot of courage for him to say that. Then he said, 'I'm not going to make excuses. I did a bad thing. Now I want to ask you to do something for me.'"

I could feel my mouth sort of hanging open, which it unfortunately does sometimes when I'm engrossed in a conversation. I shut it.

"Are you ready for the coup de grace?" Al said. She thinks she's red hot at French. Actually, I get better marks in grammar but her accent is better than mine.

"Shoot," I said.

"My father is getting married," Al said slowly, pronouncing every word carefully. "The favor is, he wants me to come to his wedding."

"Hey, that's really great," I said. "What a surprise. All along you thought it was going to be your mother."

"I told him I'd have to think about it," Al said, as if I hadn't said a word. "I told him I wasn't sure I could make it. He said he'd send me an airplane ticket and everything. I told him I'd have to let him know."

"That was pretty nervy, telling your own father you'll have to think about going to his wedding," I said.

"Well, it was pretty nervy of him to do what he did," Al said angrily. "How would you like it if your father walked out on you when you were eight years old?"

"I wouldn't," I said.

"If I go, what would I wear? What does a person wear to her father's wedding? Do you realize," Al said, pouncing on me as if I was a mouse and she was a starving cat, "that I've never in my entire existence been to a wedding?"

"Me either," I said. "People don't invite kids to weddings unless they're related, because caterers charge by the head and it gets too expensive. Your mother will buy you something to wear, I bet. Something really cool."

"If I do decide to go, I hope she doesn't buy it on sale at her store so I have to grow into it," Al said. "I haven't got much time."

"When is it?"

"A week from Saturday. He wants me to come out a few days early so I can get to know Louise and the boys. That's her name—Louise. I don't know if I like it or not," Al said.

"Is your mother invited too?" I asked.

"Of course not," Al said indignantly. "You don't invite your first wife to your second wedding. It's very bad form." She sounded just like her mother. Al can be very proper at times. Not too often, thank God.

"Sometimes you do," I said. "I've read about weddings where people do that."

"Only movie stars and actors and actresses do, as far as I know," Al said in a snippy tone of voice. "Anyway, my mother wouldn't want to go to my father's wedding. It would put her in a very awkward position."

"I guess," I said.

"Excuse me," Al said and went to the bathroom

again. "It's pretty exciting, all that's happened," she continued when she came back.

"You could've fooled me," I said. "I'd never know you were excited."

Al smiled at herself in the mirror, a big, wide smile. Then she erased it and looked stern.

"Do you think I look better when I'm smiling or when I'm serious?" she asked. She swept her bangs off her forehead and looked at herself sideways so she could see her profile.

"My nose is ridiculous," she said. "It looks as if it should belong to a wombat."

I didn't know what a wombat was, so I didn't contradict her. When most kids say something like that you know they want you to say, "Oh, no, your nose is darling," or something, but not Al. If she says her nose should belong to a wombat, she means it.

"Tell me the truth. Do you think I should go?" Al asked me seriously. "I don't know if I should or not."

"Al, I know you. You will do the right thing and go," I said, just as serious. It was a very deep moment between us. I felt like Ann Landers, giving advice. "I am your friend and I say, go."

"I will sleep on it," Al said solemnly.

"Five'll get you ten you've already decided," I said. "I know you, Al, and you'll go."

Al put her arms around my neck, which she has only done once before in her life.

"He could've got married without me," she said. "He could've just called me up after and told me he was married. But he says he wants me to be there. You've got to give him credit for that," she said.

"Yeah," I said. "And don't think he doesn't deserve a couple of points for going up to your apartment to call for you and seeing your mother after all this time."

We zapped through the living room. Teddy was watching two electric eels on TV, swimming around, recharging their own batteries. My mother and father were looking up a crossword puzzle word in the dictionary, which she said was spelled with an "a" and he said with an "e".

"Hey," I said when we were out in the hall, "that's who you can give your needlepoint eyeglass case to. Your father, for a wedding present."

"I think Ole Henry is counting on it for his birthday," Al said. She did a couple of burlesque-queen type bumps and grinds. Or maybe she was belly dancing. I couldn't tell.

"One thing about my father," Al said, poking her finger at me. "He doesn't use after-shave. Like you-know-who does. He just smells like a man. I like his smell. I noticed it right away. That and his hands. He has very nice hands. A person's smell and his hands are very important."

I knew what she meant. I liked the way Mr. Richards smelled.

Teddy opened the door. "Mom wants you," he said to me. "What're you talking about?"

"Ted," Al said, putting her hand on his shoulder, man to man. "I want to talk to you. How about finishing my needlepoint for me? There's a quarter in it for you."

"I don't think I want to," Teddy said.

"Why don't you tell him he can't finish it no matter how much he wants. You want to do it yourself," I said.

"I won't let you finish my needlepoint, Ted," Al said.

"I don't want to," Teddy said again.

"Some pal you are," Al said.

The door to her apartment down the hall opened and a man came out.

"It's him!" Al hissed. "Ole Henry!" Al's mother stood talking to Ole Henry. "There you are," she called. "It's getting late." She smiled at me. "Hello, dear," she said.

I used to be bothered that she couldn't remember my name. But now I realized it was just her way. Al says she has too much on her mind, being in Better Dresses and all.

"I'll see you in the a.m.," Al said to me, "and I will definitely *not* be wearing my brown vest."

Teddy whined, "Mom's calling you. Dad's already starting to carve," so I went into our apartment. But

I left the door open just a fraction of an inch. I wanted to get a better look at Ole Henry when he went to the elevator.

When I looked out, he'd already gone. The only way I could tell he'd been there was by the smell of after-shave lotion in the hall.

·11·

THE NEXT MORNING ON OUR WAY TO SCHOOL Al made me walk in back of her and tell her if her behind wiggled.

"If there's one thing I can't stand, it's a wiggling behind," she said. "If I thought mine did, I'd die. I might have to go on a diet."

Al used to be quite fat and wore Chubbies, which was a terrible cross for her mother to bear, as she's very chic. I followed her halfway down the block. I couldn't see her wiggling at all.

"You don't wiggle," I called to her. "You look O.K. to me." One of the doormen at 1625, a fresh dude if there ever was one, said, "You look O.K. to me too, honey." He winked at us.

"I wish I could say the same about you," Al said in

her frostiest tone of voice. We were quite pleased to see him get red in the face and turn away.

"Men have to learn their place in the world," Al said. She grabbed me by the arm. "You're sure?" she hissed. "It doesn't wiggle an iota?"

"Not one."

"Maybe I'll talk my mother into letting me get a black dress for the wedding," Al said. "Black is slimming, I understand."

"Black isn't for weddings," I told her. "It's for funerals. Boy, you'd really get off on the wrong foot if you went to your father's wedding in a black dress."

Al looked at me with respect, which happened rarely. I found it very pleasurable.

"You're right," she said slowly. "You are wise beyond your years, O skinny one."

Skinny one reminded me of yesterday. I told Al about having lunch with Polly and that next time she came to my house I'd serve my delicious peanut-butter surprise. It's an original recipe in which I take slices of bread, cut the crusts off for class, spread the bread with mayonnaise, peanut butter, and walnuts, and top the whole thing with whipped cream. It's very fattening.

"Super," Al said. "How is Polly?" I told her about Polly's sister wanting to get married to the guy she was living with and Polly's mother not wanting Evelyn to get married because he was from New

England and very proper and it wouldn't work. "I told Polly about artificial insemination," I said, "and she never even heard of it. She didn't think her mother ever heard of it either. And you know Polly's mother. There's not much she doesn't know about stuff like that. I think maybe you were pulling my leg."

"Wild," Al said, "absolutely wild. How long do bangs take to grow out, do you think?"

I could see this was going to be one of those days when Al was so engrossed in her own problems she wouldn't be able to stay away from them long.

"A couple of weeks, I guess," I said. "Maybe you could borrow one of your mother's wigs to wear to the wedding." Al's mother has three or four wigs that she keeps handy so she'll always be well groomed.

Al gave me a dirty look. "Then I really *would* look like a wombat," she said. "A fat wombat in a wig."

"A fat wombat in a black dress and a wig," I said.

Al started to laugh. "They'd take one look at me coming off the plane and start running in the opposite direction." Then she turned serious. "First impressions are very important, you know. I want those little kids to like me. I want Louise to like me. If you get right down to it, I want my father to like me. People get fed an awful lot of propaganda about teenagers these days, and, after all, he's not used to having a teen-age daughter. How does he know I'm not all spaced out and robbing poor boxes and shoplifting and all those things?"

"He doesn't," I said. "For all he knows you've got a submachine gun strapped under your jacket and you might let him have a blast if he does something you don't like."

Al stomped up the school steps as if she was mad at me. I didn't mean anything. But she was being pretty intense about her father getting married again. I guess I would be too, if I were in her shoes. It must be kind of strange, not seeing your father since you were eight years old, almost six years. When he left she was a little kid, and now she was practically a woman. Almost a woman. That must be tough. I made a mental note to treat Al with kid gloves for the next ten days. I had a feeling she was going to get more and more clutched up and by the time she was ready to hop on that airplane to take her to the wedding, she'd be ready to blow a fuse.

"Your mother," I said as we walked down the hall, "how does she feel about your father getting married again?"

Al came to a dead stop. "What do you mean, how does she feel?" she said, after a minute. "She doesn't feel anything. They've been divorced for a long time, after all."

"I just wondered," I said. "She must feel something.

Maybe she feels sad. Maybe she's jealous of Louise. Maybe she remembers when they were first married and they were happy and everything. Before you were born."

Al turned away. "I don't think they were ever happy. They used to fight a lot. I can remember hearing them fight at night, when they thought I was asleep."

"They must've been happy at first, otherwise why'd they get married at all. They must've been in love at the beginning. It stands to reason," I said. "Besides, everyone fights sometimes."

"Not the way they did," Al said. "They used to holler and call each other names and then not touch each other. I remember once, I was about seven, I guess, when my mother said, 'Alexandra, please pass the butter,' when the butter was on the table right next to my father. I got up and passed her the butter. She wouldn't even ask him."

"Well, I bet your mother feels something," I said. "Maybe this will make her marry Ole Henry faster."

"I bet your mother and father don't fight," Al said.

"Sure they do. You ought to go driving with them. My father drives so fast he usually misses the exit we want and, boy, do they fight then!" I said.

"That's not the same," Al said.

Martha Moseley stuck out her head from the door

of our homeroom. "Mr. Keogh said anyone not in their seat when the bell rings will be counted absent," she announced in her television anchorman voice. Martha is bucking to be the first woman anchorman in the business.

Al drew herself up so she looked as if she were a couple of inches taller.

"When did you have your lobotomy?" she asked Martha sweetly. "It's improved your personality one hundredfold."

One thing about Al. She reads the newspaper every day and also medical journals when she goes to the library. This gives her a decided advantage. •

"I haven't had my lobotomy yet," Martha whistled through her teeth. She was furious. "But I've had my period and that's more than some people can say."

Al broke up over that. Mr. Keogh had to get really angry and tell her to calm down. He had an announcement to make.

·12·

"AS IF I DIDN'T HAVE ENOUGH ON MY MIND," Al groaned on our way to the cafeteria. "I've got to cope with exams too. How am I going to get organized for my father's wedding and study for exams too?"

"You can do it," I said. "I have faith in you."

We got our trays and sat down next to the teachers' table. Mr. Keogh was talking to Miss Percival and Mrs. Bagg, the oldest teachers in the school. Mrs. Bagg has big dark circles under her eyes and smokes a pack of cigarettes between soup and dessert. Miss Percival has greenish white skin and gray hair. One night I had a very realistic dream. I was walking down the school corridor. It was very dark. Suddenly, my blood ran cold. There was an icy presence, although I could see no one. A wind sprang up. In the faint light from the window I could see Miss Percival floating up around the ceiling, her gray hair flowing and a pale light coming out of her skin.

Then I woke up. But since then I have always wondered about Miss Percival and what she does when she's not teaching.

"Al," Mr. Keogh called out, "I thought you might be interested to know that, starting in the fall, girls will be able to take shop." When Al first came to our school she wanted to take shop, but the principal said it was off limits for girls. Which is why Al and I and Mr. Richards made our bookshelves on our own time.

"Hey," said Al, "that's great. We've come a long way, baby." Mrs. Bagg looked a little taken aback, and Miss Percival smiled and nodded. "Don't forget to let the boys take cooking if they want." She got up and went over to the teachers' table.

"Mr. Keogh," she said, "I'm going to my father's wedding the weekend before exams. He called me up and invited me. So my mind may not be all geared up. You know? I thought I better explain in case I bomb out and fail everything."

"Don't start making excuses this far ahead, Al," Mr. Keogh said. "That's nice that you're invited to the wedding."

"You know what?" Al leaned over and looked into Mr. Keogh's face. "That's not the best part. The best part is that I inherit three brothers. And a stepmother. I don't care so much about the stepmother part. I've got a perfectly good mother of my own. But I never had any siblings, and I think I'm going to like it."

Mr. Keogh got up and shook Al's hand. "Congratulations," he said. "I think you're going to like it too. And, what's more, they're going to like you. Don't sell yourself short."

Al blinked. "That's a thought," she said. "You may be right, Mr. Keogh." She zapped back to our table.

"That Mr. Keogh is all right," she said.

Al had a date after school to go downtown to her mother's store. Her mother had arranged to have some time off so they could go shopping for a dress and shoes.

"I hate going shopping with her," Al told me. "She always wants me to wear things I wouldn't be caught dead in."

"Maybe she'll buy you something from Better Dresses," I said, joking. The idea of Al in a Better Dress was almost too much.

Al tossed her bangs out of her face.

"Actually," she said, "maybe that wouldn't be such a bad idea. I think I'm going to be one of those women who looks older than she is. I've led a full life, and the other night I noticed a few lines around my eyes."

I poked her in the stomach. "You probably forgot to wash your face," I said, laughing.

Al turned on me, her eyes blazing, her cheeks red.

"It's all right for you to fool around," she said at the top of her voice. "You don't understand. You're just a little wimp with a ready-made family. You don't realize how important it is, getting one for the first time. Just don't joke about something that's totally foreign to you, all right?"

I started to say I was sorry. Then I got mad.

"Don't take yourself so seriously," I said. "You're not the first person who ever went to her father's wedding. I know plenty of people whose fathers and mothers are divorced and get married again and everything. Don't think it makes you so special, because it doesn't."

We didn't talk to each other for the rest of the afternoon. When the bell rang, Al shot out the door. She must've got a bus right away, because when I got out onto the street she was nowhere in sight.

· 13 ·

TALK ABOUT KID GLOVES. I GUESS I DIDN'T DO a very good job of handling Al with them. We'd only fought once before, when I made a dopey remark about how fathers thought daughters were something special. All Al ever got from her father were postcards and, once in a while, a ten dollar check.

Maybe I'd go to her apartment after supper and pretend nothing had happened. Maybe I would. I'd have to think about it.

The doorbell rang—two, then one, then two. That was Al's special ring.

"What do you think?" she asked, looking down at me.

"Holy Toledo!" I said. "Where'd you get those?"

"Aren't they super?" Her shoes were red and they

had soles about four inches thick and big clunky heels. She staggered into the living room. "They take a bit of getting used to," she explained. "My mother and I made a deal. She said if she bought me these shoes, which make her hair stand on end, then she could choose the dress. I said O.K."

She knelt down and wiped her new shoes with a scruffy piece of Kleenex. "I love them," she said. "I really love them. I never thought I could love a pair of shoes. Can I look at them in the full-length mirror?"

"Sure," I said.

Al clumped down the hall into my mother's room. She turned this way and that, admiring her shoes from every angle.

"I'm sorry I called you a wimp," she said. "You're not one. I was just sore."

"That's all right," I said. "You want a shooter of Coke?"

"I'm on a diet," Al said firmly. "Think thin. Now all I have to do is get a present for my father and Louise. My mother suggested place mats. Place mats, for creep's sake. I was thinking more along the lines of a silver bowl. Or a silver ashtray. My mother says she can't afford silver. I think she plain doesn't want to afford silver." She looked at her watch. "I better get going. Ole Henry's coming for dinner."

She took off one of her shoes and scratched her

foot. "You know something? I'm sorry you asked about how my mother feels about my father getting married again."

"Why?" I said.

"Because you put the idea in my head. Maybe you're right. She was talking today about a friend of hers who got divorced from her husband, then she turned around a year later and married him again. Oh, well," Al shrugged. "Too late now. The fat's in the fire."

I watched Al clump down the hall in her new shoes. They made her walk sort of like Frankenstein. They also made her behind wiggle. Just a little. Maybe I better tell her. But on second thought, no.

A man got out of the elevator.

"Hello, Mr. Lynch," Al said.

"What's this?" Ole Henry did a double take. He blinked up at her. Those shoes made Al almost as tall as a basketball player.

"You're turning into a fine young lady," he said. He reached out to pat Al on the head. His arm was too short. He patted her on the shoulder instead.

"My, my, you certainly have grown," he said.

·14·

THAT NIGHT AL SLEPT WITH HER SHOES tucked under her pillow.

"I didn't sleep very well," she told me next morning. "They were awfully lumpy. But every time I woke up I reached under to make sure they were there. I'll probably grow up having a shoe fetish."

What I should do is carry a small notebook around, and every time Al uses a word I don't understand, I should write it down to look up when I get home. I should, but I know I never will.

"Do you think I should kiss them?" Al said. I didn't think she meant her shoes. "Not when I get there. That's too soon. But when I leave. Of course I'll kiss my father and maybe Louise. Women kiss each other more. But the boys. I don't know."

"Play it by ear," I said.

After school Al went home and had a couple of trial runs on her shoes.

"They're coming," she said later. "Slow but sure."

"Maybe you should turn on a record and practice walking around in time to the music," I said. "Hold your arms out like those showgirls we saw in that old movie last week."

Al's eyes lighted up. "Yeah, I could practice walking down the service stairs balancing a book on my head. Maybe Mr. Ogilvy would hold the door open into the lobby and I could walk right through and out onto the street."

"That'd really shake some people up," I said.

"Listen, you want to come shopping with me today?" Al asked. "My mother gave me her charge plate. She said I could send a dress home, only she reserves the right to return it if she doesn't like it." Al made a face. "I think what she has in mind is something that will make me look like Rebecca of Sunnybrook Farm."

"My mother's big on smocking," I said. "She says I used to look adorable in my little smocked dresses with matching panties. 'It's too bad girls don't dress like that any more. All they wear is jeans.'"

"My mother thinks it's a pity that jeans have taken over the earth," Al agreed.

Going shopping with Al was an experience. We must've covered every junior miss, teen, and young sophisticate department in town. Each dress Al tried on was worse than the last. Every time she got one zipped up and looked at herself in the mirror, she'd become more depressed.

"I look as if I'm six months' pregnant in this one," she said, puffing out her cheeks and crossing her eyes at herself.

The saleslady, who wasn't sure whether we would rip off a few garments if she turned her back, made little cooing noises.

"You look perfectly sweet," she said firmly.

Al peered out from a ruff of white organdy.

"You know who you look like?" I said. "Mary Queen of Scots."

"That does it," Al said. "What I need is to look like Mary Queen of Scots. Rebecca of Sunnybrook Farm isn't enough."

The saleslady had given up the idea of making a sale. She gathered up all of the rejected finery.

"When I was your age," she said, "girls wanted to look feminine and pretty, not like hooligans."

"What's a hooligan?" Al asked her, taking off her Mary Queen of Scots outfit.

The lady pretended she hadn't heard. She glided off in the pursuit of fresher prospects.

We started down on the escalator. On the third floor, Al spied a sort of one-shouldered, blue beach dress on a model.

"How much is that?" she asked the salesman.

"I beg your pardon?" the man said.

"How much is that dress?" Al pointed to it.

"I don't work here," the man said apologetically. "I'm waiting for my wife."

"I can't stand the kind of man who waits while his wife tries on clothes," Al said as we zapped back on the escalator. "I'm not going to marry the kind of man who'll do that. If I feel like buying a tangerine-colored G-string, I'll go ahead and buy it and not have my husband approve."

"You'd be a smash in one of those," I said. We stopped at the hat bar to try on a few hats. I found a green one with a feather that wasn't bad. A Robin Hood hat. Al tried on a black job with a big floppy brim. She pulled it down on either side of her face and sucked in her cheeks.

"Alms for the poor," she said in a sing-song.

"Get lost," a voice said.

The girl behind the counter was a vision. Her eye liner was coordinated with her eye shadow, which was coordinated with her nail polish.

We took off the hats.

"Who said that?" Al asked, looking around. "It couldn't have been her," she said, pointing to the girl, "because I don't think she's real. She's made of plastic. They do wonderful things with plastic these days."

We both stared.

"I said get lost, you two," the girl said out of one corner of her mouth.

"I'm going to bring George—that's my husband, George—back to try on that black hat for him," Al said to me. "I do hope when I bring him they have somebody to wait on us. It's terrible, the lack of salespeople today."

Al and I sailed off and went through the revolving door twice on our way out.

·15·

AL'S FATHER SENT THE AIRPLANE TICKET.
First class.

"I usually go tourist," she said, smiling. She has
been on an airplane lots of times. I never have.

Her ticket looked as if the moths had been at it. She
took it to school every day in her wallet, in case
somebody broke into her apartment in search of
valuables. She read the fine print at night to make
sure there weren't any catches. She said she didn't
trust first class.

"Ta-dah!" Three nights in a row Al said this when
I answered the door. Each time she wore a dress her
mother had sent home.

"Maybe I should've settled for looking like Mary
Queen of Scots, six months' pregnant," she said.

"That one's not bad," I said.

"It makes me look waistless," she said. She was right.

"Your bangs are practically gone," I said to cheer her up. It was true. They'd grown enough so she could hold them back with a barette. "You have a nice forehead."

"Listen, I think I'll put that on my tombstone," she said. "Here lies Al. She had a nice forehead."

"You're awfully sour. How come you're so sour these days?" I asked her. For almost the first time since I'd known her she wasn't fun to be with. I couldn't joke and kid around with her without her taking things the wrong way and getting her back up. I'd be glad when Al's father and Louise were safely married.

Al sat down on my bed and put her head in her hands.

"I know," she said in a muffled voice. "The way I'm carrying on about what I wear is ridiculous. How shallow can you get? I remind myself of Martha Moseley and others of her ilk. I could kill myself when I get like that. It's just that if I come off the plane looking like a sack of potatoes, that's the way they'll always think of me . . . a sack of potatoes."

I didn't know what to say.

Al looked at me.

"You know what?" she said. "Last night I heard

my mother crying. She thought I was asleep. I'm a very light sleeper. I heard her get up and get a glass of water. Then she turned off the light and I heard her. She cried for a long time."

Al started pacing around the edges of my rug. She only does this when things are bad.

"One thing about my mother. She's not the crying type. I saw her cry only once before. And that was when my grandmother, her mother, died."

And I had to go and open my big mouth. Maybe Al's mother was still in love with Al's father and she'd been planning on marrying him again, like her friend remarried her husband. But now he was going to marry somebody else.

"Maybe I shouldn't go," Al said. "Maybe I should send the airplane ticket back and tell them I broke my leg or had my appendix out unexpectedly."

For once I took charge.

"You'd spoil it for everybody if you did that," I said. "You'd spoil it for your father and Louise and the boys. They're expecting you. You want to really louse things up? Pull yourself together," I said firmly.

Even to myself, I sounded like my mother. It's a terrible thing when you're twelve and a half and you already sound like your own mother. It makes you stop and think.

· 16 ·

"ONE THING I POSITIVELY DRAW THE LINE at," Al said, "and that's gloves. My mother's putting the moves on me to wear a pair of stupid white gloves. 'At least until you get off the plane, dear'," Al said, mimicking her mother. "I think she thinks maybe Louise won't think I'm a first-class citizen if I don't wear white gloves." She snorted in disgust. "Sometimes I think my mother thinks it's the nineteenth century. She has some nineteenth century ideas."

Her mother finally brought home a dress they both liked, a red-and-white check, to go with the shoes.

"Isn't it super?" Al tried her whole outfit on for me. "I feel put together. It's the first time I ever felt that way." She put a new Band-Aid on each heel. Due to the fact that she'd increased her practice time, her new shoes had given her gigantic blisters.

"I feel like a baby learning to walk all over again," she said.

"Try it on your hands and knees," I suggested.

"Listen, if these blisters get any bigger, maybe I will." She studied her profile. "I may save up for plastic surgery," she said.

"Don't forget to send me a postcard," I told her.

"If I have time. I'll get there Thursday afternoon, the wedding's Saturday, and I come back Sunday morning." Al was being excused from school all of Thursday and Friday. Her mother had talked to the principal, explaining the situation so Al could get off.

"I'm going to study on the plane," she said.

I gave her the fishy eyeball. "Al," I said, "you are talking to somebody who knows you. I am not one to be taken in by lies and hallucinations."

"Sorry about that," Al said. "I thought I was talking to my mother."

"Are you afraid to go up in a plane?" I asked her. I would love to fly but something tells me I'd be scared. I heard my grandmother telling once how afraid she was to go to the ladies' room the whole way to Minneapolis for fear that if she walked down the aisle she might make the plane tip. I think that's the way I'd feel. But I'd like to have a chance to find out.

"It's kind of spooky when the plane first takes off," she said. "It's exciting but spooky too."

"I've got a good idea," I said, "take your needle-point along to calm your nerves."

"Right," Al said. "Listen, I have a favor to ask." She gave me a piercer, so I knew it was something serious.

"Sure," I said. "Ask away."

"I want you to go over to my apartment after I'm gone," she said. "Just to see if my mother wants anything. O.K.? She might get lonely or something, though I doubt it. Probably the minute the plane takes off, Ole Henry will put his feet up on the coffee table and start playing gin rummy. He plays an awful lot of gin rummy."

"If you want," I said. I had never been alone with Al's mother. I mean, Al was always with me. When you have a friend, you usually don't talk to your friend's mother. Not really talk. She might ask you how your mother and father are or if you're over your cold, but that's all. Plus the fact that Al's mother only calls me "dear."

"She might not even be home," Al went on, "but I'd feel better if I know you're around in case she wants anything."

"Polly might come over on Saturday," I said. "But even if she does, we can go over."

Polly can talk to anyone. I guess that comes from having your father in the diplomatic service and living in different places. You get to have poise. Polly could tell Al's mother about Evelyn wanting to get married when she went to Boston and about how her mother wanted to change her name back to what it was before she got married. She could tell about wanting to be a really great chef. When you come right down to it, Polly was a lot more interesting than most people.

Al's mother sent a crystal vase to Al's father and Louise for a wedding present. Al told me it was real crystal. You could tell by flicking it with your finger. If it sang, that was crystal.

"They're going to live in the country," Al said, "so it figures they'll have a lot of flowers. My mother says no one ever has enough vases. Especially crystal ones."

Al had her knapsack all packed and ready four days before she was supposed to go. Then her mother went out and bought her a suitcase stamped with her initials.

"It's kind of square," she said, "but O.K., I guess. You know what she said when she saw my knapsack? She said, 'People will think we don't know any better.' You know who people is, right? Louise, that's who. My mother's all hung up on middle-class values."

"You sound exactly like Polly when you say that," I said.

Al looked surprised. "I do?" she said.

On Wednesday night, Al came over to say good-bye.

"Well, I'm off first thing in the morning," she said nonchalantly.

"Where ya going?" Teddy asked.

Teddy could be in the midst of a hurricane and say, "Wind? What wind?" Or he could be caught in a bank when somebody tried to rob it and say, "I didn't hear any guns going off." He must inherit this tendency from my father who tunes people and things out if his mind is busy elsewhere. Al had been talking about going to her father's wedding only for almost two weeks straight, night and day.

"My father's wedding," Al told Teddy.

He snuffled. Probably if he'd been alone, he'd pick his nose. "No kidding? I thought your father was already married," Teddy said.

My mother kissed Al good-bye. "Have a lovely time," she said. "We'll be waiting to hear all about it."

"Don't forget," Al said when we were out in the hall. "About my mother, I mean."

"I won't," I promised. "Take it easy on the champagne."

Al did a little belly dance.

"Have a weird day," she said.

"You too," I told her.

I watched her walk down the hall to her apartment. When she was almost there, I opened our door and went in so I wouldn't have to say good-bye again.

· 17 ·

WHEN I CALLED POLLY FRIDAY NIGHT, HER mother said she was running a fever of a hundred and three and couldn't come.

"I suspect it may be measles," she told me. "There's a lot of it around and she's never had them."

I said I was sorry. I was. Not only because Polly might have the measles but because that meant I'd have to go see Al's mother alone.

"You want me to do the wash?" I asked my mother Saturday morning. She looked at me in surprise.

"I hadn't really thought," she said. "I haven't worked my way beyond tonight's dinner. Why do you ask?"

My mother is the kind of housekeeper who has to do things spontaneously. If she happens to feel like running the vacuum, she runs it. But if she happens to feel like writing a letter or reading a magazine, that comes first.

"Because Al asked me if I'd check in and see if her mother was all right, if she needed anything. She's worried about her, I guess. I thought if I had to do the wash, then I couldn't stay too long," I said.

"Hey," my mother said, "I like that, the child worrying about the parent. That's a nice twist. Go check under Teddy's bed. You'll strike it rich."

I went into his room. It smelled. Of quite a few things.

"Get under the bed and bring out whatever you can carry," I told him. He was halfway under before he realized he was being bossed around. He started to back out, mouth open to moan and carry on. I strategically placed a sharp knitting needle against his rump. I carry this needle around for just such purposes.

"Don't make any sudden moves," I told him, "or I may draw blood."

He crawled back in, muttering and groaning as he worked his way through the old apple cores and orange peels. My mother said she has too many other things to do than to check under our beds for debris. That was our responsibility, she said. My mother is trying to bring Teddy and me up to be responsible citizens. It isn't easy, as she'll tell you at the drop of a hat.

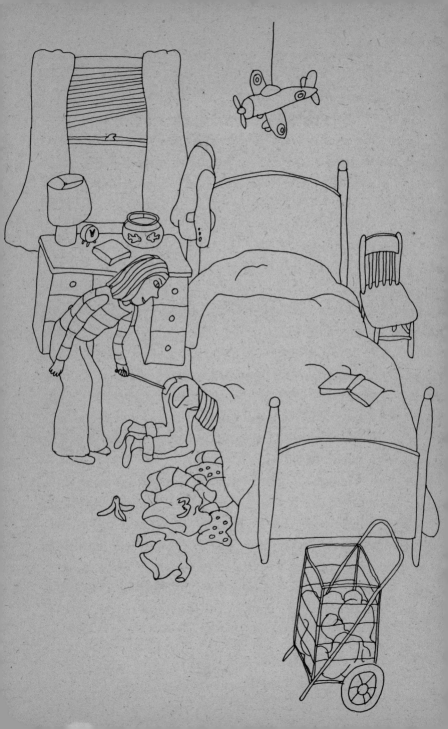

I managed to half fill a laundry bag.

"I guess I'll go over now," I said.

"That'll be a nice gesture," my mother said, lying on the couch reading a book.

"You ought to be the one to go," I said. "She's more your age than she is mine."

"A good point," my mother said. "Let me read you this. It's a riot."

She knows if there's one thing that drives me bonkers it's to be read to from a book somebody else likes. I went down the hall to Al's apartment.

I rang the bell. Maybe she wouldn't be home. Sometimes she had Saturdays off, sometimes not. If no one answered, I could always say I'd tried.

"Why, hello, dear," Al's mother said when she opened the door. She seemed quite glad to see me.

"Come in and have a sandwich." She didn't even ask me what I was doing there. She seemed to accept me as a person, not like a friend of her kid's. Before I knew what I was doing, I was sitting at the kitchen table while she made us both a bologna sandwich. I was relieved to see she used mayonnaise instead of butter, also that she put both mustard and relish on without asking. You can tell all kinds of things about a person by the way she makes a bologna sandwich.

"What fun!" she said. "I was going through our old photograph albums when you came. Now we can do it together. There are lots of pictures of Alexandra when she was a baby, when we lived in California, outside of L.A."

When Al first came to our apartment house, she told me she had lived in L.A., among other places. I thought she meant Ellay. I told her I never heard of a place called Ellay. She didn't even laugh at me. I thought that was nice of her.

"I'm filled with nostalgia today," Al's mother said. "I guess it's because Al's at her father's wedding." She looked at her watch. "They must be having the ceremony just about now. I do hope she has a good time. You know, it seems like only yesterday that Al looked like that." She put a mess of pictures in front of me.

All I can say is, Al was a pretty funny-looking baby. She's much better-looking now.

"I'll never forget how I felt when my mother-in-law came to the hospital to see Al," she went on. "It was her first grandchild. I said, 'I'm warning you, she isn't a pretty baby. In fact, she's funny-looking.' I guess I wanted her to be prepared. Anyway, when she came back from the nursery, she said, 'I'm not going to lie to you, she *is* funny-looking.'"

Al's mother took our plates and put them in the sink. "And do you know, I cried for a long time after she left. My husband was furious at her, but what could he do? The damage had been done. I've never forgotten it." She smiled at me.

"What a stinky thing to say," I told her.

"Yes," she agreed, "it *was* stinky. She was an extraordinarily tactless woman."

We settled down to look at the pictures. The door-bell rang and Al's mother said, "Oh, dear, that's probably Mr. Lynch. When she opened the door, she said, "Hello, Henry." She didn't sound overjoyed to see him. "You know Al's little friend. We were just looking at some photographs."

"I thought you might be in need of some company today," Ole Henry said. "Thought you might be a bit lonely, Al gone and all."

"That was kind of you," Al's mother said. "I might have, but we've been having a fine time, talking and looking at these old photographs. There's nothing like looking at old photographs to bring back memories."

She went to the kitchen and made him a sandwich. Then the three of us looked at the pictures.

"There's Al and her father and me in the park. Look at the length of that dress, will you! And the hair! You see that bonnet Al's wearing? Some old lady knitted it and I didn't want to offend her, so I put it on Al. It was pink. Her father said she looked like Barney Oldfield in it. He was a racing driver," she said to me.

We looked at lots more pictures, she and I. Ole Henry got bored. He walked around the room, whistling under his breath.

"Oh, what fun we had in those days," Al's mother said. "We did nothing but laugh. Life was marvelous." She turned the last page and we sat and said nothing.

"There's nothing like your first love, I guess," she said quietly. I think she was talking to me.

Ole Henry put his hand on hers.

"Each of my wives has been very dear to me," he said. "Each dearer than the last."

Holy Toledo, how many wives had he had? I made a mental note to tell Al to find out.

Just call him Bluebeard Lynch.

"I better get going," I said. "Thanks for the sandwich."

"You were sweet to come see me." Al's mother walked me to the door. "I enjoyed it more than I can say."

"Same here," I said. I meant it.

"I expect Alexandra will be over first thing tomorrow to tell you about the wedding," she said.

"Tell her I'll be waiting," I said.

She shut the door and I pushed the elevator button for down before I realized I didn't have my laundry bag. I was just reaching to ring her bell again, although I didn't want to, when the door opened.

"You forgot this," Al's mother said.

I said thank you. I'd forgotten my excuse for getting away. I hadn't needed it, after all.

· 18 ·

AL CALLED ME ABOUT EIGHT O'CLOCK SATUR-
day night.

"Hey baby," she said, "it's me."

"Where are you? You're not home already, are
you?" I said.

"Of course not, dope. I'm at the wedding. I have
to talk fast because they'll probably want me downstairs any minute. I asked Louise if I could use the
phone. I charged the call to our number. You can do
that, you know. My mother will blow a fuse, probably. I couldn't wait to get home to tell you about it.
It was the most fun. You wouldn't believe how great
it was. The three little kids, my stepbrothers, are some
super kids. They are named Chris and Nick and Sam.
They have a pig and two cows and a barn. They grow

practically all the food they eat, and they asked me to come back this summer and stay. I said I'd have to see. They had champagne at the wedding, and I took my shoes off. Those shoes really got to me. Nobody minded. They had a cake that a friend of Louise's baked, with a little house made of sugar on top. My father took me around and introduced me to all his friends. 'This is my daughter, Al,' he said. If I'm talking a lot, it's probably because I had two glasses of champagne."

"Who said you're talking a lot?" I managed to get in.

"Well, when you're calling long distance you don't want to waste a penny, right? Anyway," Al went on, "as I said, I couldn't wait to tell you all about it. They like me. I really think they like me a lot. They're very nice people. Maybe I can bring you with me when I come back. I met this kid. I'll have to tell you about him when I get home. Louise made the dress she wore. It was beautiful. It was like thistles. My favorite stepbrother is Sam, I think. He's seven. I took a whole bunch of pictures. I'll bring them home and get them developed. . . . Yeah, O.K., I'm coming. I've got to go, they're calling for me to come downstairs," Al said. "But there's just one more thing."

"What's that?" My voice sounded sort of hoarse. I hadn't used it in so long.

"I got my period," Al said.

"No kidding! Terrific!" I said.

There was a pause. I could hear voices in the background.

"It's not so much," Al said, "See you." And she hung up.

·19·

"THEY ALL KISSED ME AT THE AIRPORT, EVEN Chris and he's ten, which is a little old for kissing."

Al had gone to her apartment, changed her clothes and zapped over to see me. She took up where she'd left off the night before. If I closed my eyes, I'd think she was still on the telephone.

"What's Louise look like?" I got in.

"Louise? Well, she's not too tall, about as tall as me, and she's sort of tender looking. She had this really low voice and she never hollers at the boys. They do what she wants. I think Sam is my favorite. He's seven. He's so cute. I took scads of pictures."

"When'd you get your period?" I asked.

"Right before the wedding. That was lucky. No problem. It was like a fire drill at school. You know, you've practiced so much you know exactly what to do. My mother had packed my period readiness kit and, zap, there I was, all set."

"Who's the kid you met?" I asked her.

"What kid?"

"The one you mentioned over the phone. You said you'd tell me when you got home."

"Oh, him." Al looked at her sneakers. "He's fifteen. He said he might write me. I don't think he will."

"Did you give him your address?" I said.

"Yeah, I wrote it on a piece of paper. He'll probably lose it."

"He's nice," I said, not asking her.

"He's all right." Al's eyes were very bright. "He mows Louise's lawn for her. His parents are friends of hers. He'd had a glass of champagne when he asked me for my address. Which is probably why he asked. So had I. Two."

"You told me."

"His name's Brian," Al said.

I looked at my fingernails. "I went over to see your mother," I said. "We looked at baby pictures of you. I had a good time."

"She told me," Al said. "Thanks a lot."

"I never really talked to her before," I told her. "I enjoyed it. She made us a bologna sandwich. Ole Henry came over and she made him one too. I don't think she's red hot on him."

"I'm going to have to talk to my mother more," Al said. "She and I don't communicate enough. I feel different, since I've been to the wedding. You know how you worry and worry about something, the way I worried about the wedding? You want things to be perfect, but you know that almost nothing is ever perfect. Almost nothing lives up to expectations. But this wedding, the whole thing, was exactly what I hoped for. Nothing will ever be so perfect again. It's like something I can take and hold in my hand and look at once in a while. You know?"

I nodded, although I didn't really know.

"I've been thinking." Al got up and started to pace.

"Don't give me that," I said. "I know I'm gullible but I draw the line somewhere."

"I've decided my father is far from the ideal father," Al said, without smiling at my joke. "He did go off and not see me for six years, right?"

I kept quiet.

"Not only that," she continued, "he also walked out on my mother and left her to take the full burden of raising a child."

I wondered who Al was quoting. Probably Ole Henry. It sounded like something he'd say.

"I know he sent me money and postcards, but what are money and postcards compared to the day-to-day stuff?"

"I don't know," I said.

"Zilch, that's what," Al said. "Nothing but zilch."

"I don't think I'll ever forgive my father completely for what he did," Al went on. "I think I understand him better now, and maybe when I'm old I'll appreciate him more. Still, he shouldn't have gone off and left me, then snap his fingers and expect me to jump."

Al snapped her fingers. They barely made any noise at all. I've always been good at snapping my fingers. I can make a really loud noise. I can also make a loud noise when I put a piece of grass between my thumbs and blow. Not too many people can do that.

She sat down beside me and we both stared out the window.

After the silence had dragged on a bit, I said, "But it turned out really well, right? Better than you planned. You like them, they like you."

"Yeah," Al said, "but then I keep thinking of Mr. Richards."

"Why?" I asked.

"Remember how he told us his wife took their baby daughter back home, and when he tried to send them money, his wife sent it back. He never saw his grandchildren. Why?"

Al gave me a real piercer. I knew better than to interrupt.

"I'll tell you why. His daughter wouldn't forgive *him*, either, for walking out on her. I think people who never forgive are crumby. It's a terrible thing to never forgive something, even if it hurt you a lot. Don't you think so?" Al said.

"Yes," I said. The only thing I ever had to really forgive was when Teddy flushed my silver ring down the toilet by mistake. I still haven't forgiven him, but he doesn't know it.

"So I'm going to try to forgive my father," Al said, getting up. "The older I get, the more I know that not only is almost nothing perfect, but almost nobody, no person, is either."

"Sometimes I think that thee and me are the only perfect ones," I said, "and once in a while I worry about thee."

"Have a weird day," Al said, and went home.

· 20 ·

PEOPLE EXPECT GRANDFATHERS TO BE SORT OF dried up and crotchety. My grandfather is very hand-some. He is my mother's father. My grandmother, his wife, died before I was born. He always stands up when a lady comes into the room. Even one my age.

"Remember that cleft chin? If you want to see one," I told Al after gym, "come over about six. My grandfather's coming. You said to let you know."

I didn't tell her about the standing up. I knew that would get her. I like to watch Al's face when she's surprised. She has a very expressive face.

My grandfather has a lot of dates, for a man his age. This time he brought Mrs. Oakley, who has been to our house before. She is very dainty and scented and wears a hat and gloves and pale clothes. I have never seen anyone like her. My father calls her a "*grande dame*," Only he pronounces it in French, which makes it sound considerably different.

Mrs. Oakley sits with her ankles crossed. She handles a teacup so it seems part of her. She's nice to me, but she's one of those ladies who gives the men her full attention. She turns the old eyes on my father or my grandfather when they talk to her like she has never seen or met anyone so fascinating. Her hands look as if she never did a day's work in her life. My mother says she probably hasn't. My mother isn't all that hot on Mrs. Oakley. My father thinks she's a great old girl. My grandfather seems to be amused by her. Teddy acts like some kind of a retard when Mrs. Oakley's around. More than usual, I mean.

I noticed my mother had on a new skirt and a new blouse. My father had come home from work and put on a clean shirt. Mrs. Oakley has that effect on people. My mother gave my father the hairy eyeball and made a couple of remarks about not seeing any clean shirts for her.

"I asked Al to come over," I told my mother. "She has never seen a cleft chin."

When Al came, I introduced her to Mrs. Oakley and to my grandfather.

"Grandfather," I said, "this is my friend Al."

He stood up. I saw Al get a little pink in the face.

"What's Al short for?" he asked her, shaking her hand.

"Alexandra," she said.

"When you're older, you'll probably be glad of Alexandra," he said. "You know me, Al."

We looked at each other, confused.

"I know *you*, Al," I said.

"You two are old enough to read Ring Lardner," my grandfather said. "He wrote a book of pieces about some very interesting characters. He called it *You Know Me, Al*. Give it a whirl. You might like it."

Al and I went into the kitchen. My mother had asked me if I'd turn on the broiler and watch the little toast things so they wouldn't burn.

"He's super," Al said. She stationed herself at the window in the kitchen door that maids looked through when people had maids. I knew without looking at her that she was shooting a few of her special piercers at the folks out there.

"Who's she?" Al asked.

I knew who she meant. "She's just a lady who's a friend of my grandfather's," I said. "He brings a lot of different ladies when he comes."

"She looks as if she might break if you dropped her," Al said in a sour voice.

"Get me the silver plate, will you?" I asked Al. She knows the plate I mean. My mother keeps it in a special wrapper so it won't tarnish.

Al tore herself away from the peephole and got the plate. She watched me as I opened the oven door.

"I read something very interesting in the paper the other day," she said. "Did you know it's a proven fact that people can enjoy sex well into their seventies and eighties?"

I almost dropped the toast things.

"It's true," Al said. "I was amazed. Isn't that bizarre? A bunch of doctors made a scientific study, and those were their conclusions."

Al stationed herself at the peephole again.

"Does your grandfather like her?" she said.

"He likes the opposite sex," I said.

"I'm going to read that book he suggested," Al said.

"I know you, Al," I said.

"No, it's *You Know Me Al*," she corrected.

Sometimes she could be awfully literal. "In my case, it's 'I know you, Al,'" I said. "Hold the door for me, will you?"

"What a fine young man you've turned into, Teddy," Mrs. Oakley was saying. "I'd never would have known you, you've grown so big and strong."

As I say, keep a foot in the middle of Teddy's back and beat him regularly and he stays in line. Give him a word of encouragement and he takes off. Teddy was revving his engines for takeoff.

"I've got a song I can sing for you," he said.

Al and I froze.

I passed the hors d'oeuvres so fast they skidded and almost hit the dirt.

"That would be lovely," Mrs. Oakley said in her dainty voice. "Both my brothers sang. In the church choir. They had lovely voices. There's nothing sweeter in the world than a young boy singing. I can still see them in their choir robes, their faces so young, so innocent. Lovely."

Mrs. Oakley took a toast round.

Al and I escaped to the kitchen.

Al opened the door to the broom closet and went in. "Call me when it's over," she said.

"You really want me to sing?" I heard Teddy ask. I looked through the peephole. My mother had a little puzzled smile on her face. She hadn't known Teddy sang. My father and grandfather looked noncommittal. Mrs. Oakley smiled. She was prepared to enjoy herself and give Teddy a big hand when he finished.

I turned on the water, both taps, as hard as I could. Even above the noise I could hear Teddy begin.

"My bonnie lies over the ocean," he sang. "My bonnie lies over the sea."

I couldn't stand it another minute. I opened the door to the broom closet. Al had her hands over her mouth. Her face was beet red. It was a very small broom closet.

"Move over," I said.

About the Author

CONSTANCE C. GREENE is one of the leading comic writers for young people. A native New Yorker, she attended Skidmore College and worked for the Associated Press before her marriage. Mrs. Greene and her husband, who are the parents of five grown children, live in Poland Spring, Maine.

I Know You, Al continues the story of *A Girl Called Al*.